Elfelyn and her fairy friends

For Sebastian, my ray of light.

Elfelyn and her fairy friends,

Live in an enchanted forest, green.

With wings of gold and silver,

The most magical ever seen.

Her long locks are golden brown,

And eyes are aqua blue,

She has a tiny nose that twitches,

Before sneezing, as if on cue!

Peril and Luna share her home,

High up in the forest tree,

Keeping watch over their kingdom,

On the look-out for Grentalie….

Grentalie was a fairy once,

But jealousy turned her green.

She started the 'green army of the exiled',

To be banished by the fairy Queen.

Fairies forage for fairy supplies,

To mystical music and bells by day.

At night is when the trouble comes,

And Grentalie's army comes out to play.

They steal food and set fire to trees,

Causing havoc among the night sky.

Fairy doors are locked and bolted tight,

Some fairies abandon home and fly.

However, the fairy Queen’s Royal Army,

Are on guard and ready to fight!

Using fairy dust to extinguish fires,

Fending off Grentalie with all their might!

As morning dawns, the forest settles,

The green army have made their retreat.

All damage is fixed by the fairies,

And more food gathered to eat.

Grentalie’s actions are mean,

But the fairies do not let her ‘win’.

For they know that she is bitter,

And unhappy in her green skin.

They would rather stay home in the forest,

Risking a visit from the army of green,

Than give up their enchanted land,

Living happily by the magical stream.

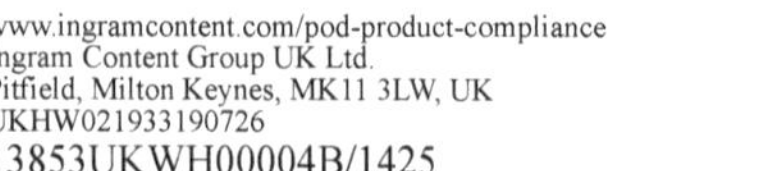
www.ingramcontent.com/pod-product-compliance
Ingram Content Group UK Ltd.
Pitfield, Milton Keynes, MK11 3LW, UK
UKHW021933190726
13853UKWH00004B/1425

9 798801 964881